SIMON & SCHUSTER BOOKS FOR YOUNG READERS

An imprint of Simon & Schuster Children's Publishing Division

1230 Avenue of the Americas, New York, New York 10020

SIMON & SCHUSTER BOOKS FOR YOUNG READERS is a trademark of Simon & Schuster, Inc.

For information about special discounts for bulk purchases, please contact Simon &
Schuster Special Sales at 1-866-506-1949 or business@simonandschuster.com.

The Simon & Schuster Speakers Bureau can bring authors to your live event.

For more information or to book an event, contact the Simon & Schuster

Speakers Bureau at 1-866-248-3049 or visit our website at www.simonspeakers.com.

Book design by Alice Provensen

The text for this book is set in Futura.

The illustrations for this book are rendered in oils.

Manufactured in China

0815 SCP

10 9 8 7 6 5 4 3 2 1

Library of Congress Cataloging-in-Publication Data

Provensen, Alice, author, illustrator.

Murphy in the city / Alice Provensen ; illustrations by Alice Provensen

with the assistance of Jody Wheeler. — 1st edition.

pages cm

Companion to: A day in the life of Murphy.

Summary: Murphy, a small terrier, reluctantly leaves his farm for a trip to the city, where he finds many
things to do—and bark at—but he is happy to return to his barn at the end of the day.

ISBN 978-1-4424-1971-1 (hardback) — ISBN 978-1-4814-1832-4 (eBook)

1. Terriers—Juvenile fiction. [1. Terriers—Fiction. 2. Dogs—Fiction. 3. City and town life—Fiction.
4. Humorous stories.] I. Wheeler, Jody, illustrator. II. Title.

PZ10.3.P928Mur 2015

[E]—dc23

2015005872

MURPHY
IN THE CITY

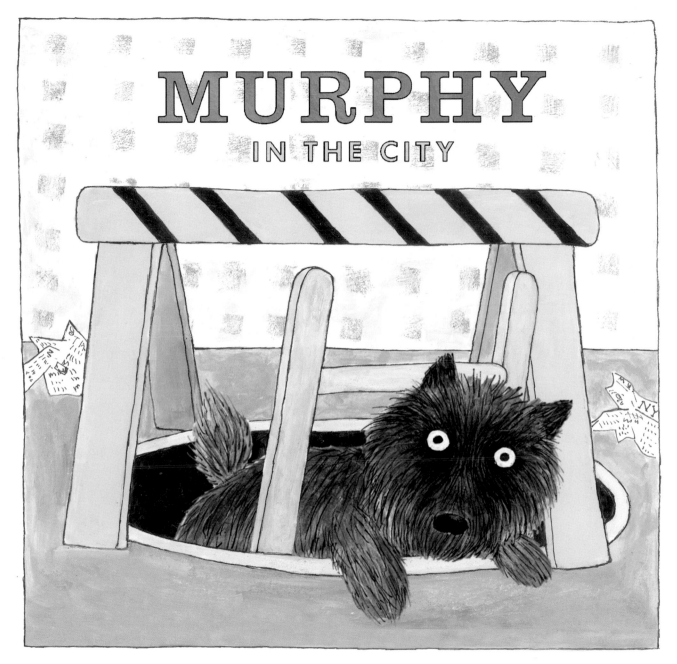

Alice Provensen

SIMON & SCHUSTER BOOKS FOR YOUNG READERS

New York   London · Toronto   Sydney   New Delhi

MY NAME IS MURPHY-STOP-THAT.
I AM A SMALL TERRIER.
I LIVE ON A FARM.
I BARK A LOT.

BECAUSE I'M SO NOISY,
I HAVE TO SLEEP IN THE BARN WITH ALL THE BIG
DUMB FARM ANIMALS.

A HONKING HORN WOKE ME UP.

I'M CURIOUS. WHAT'S GOING ON?

OH! OH! IT WAS HONKING FOR ME!
I SHOULD HAVE GONE INTO HIDING!

I **HATE** TO RIDE IN THE CAR. IT MAKES
ME SICK!

SMELLS OF GAS! GREASY OIL!

IF I PUT MY HEAD OUT THE WINDOW,
THINGS BLOW IN MY EYES.

WELL, I GUESS I'M GOING WHETHER I WANT TO OR NOT.

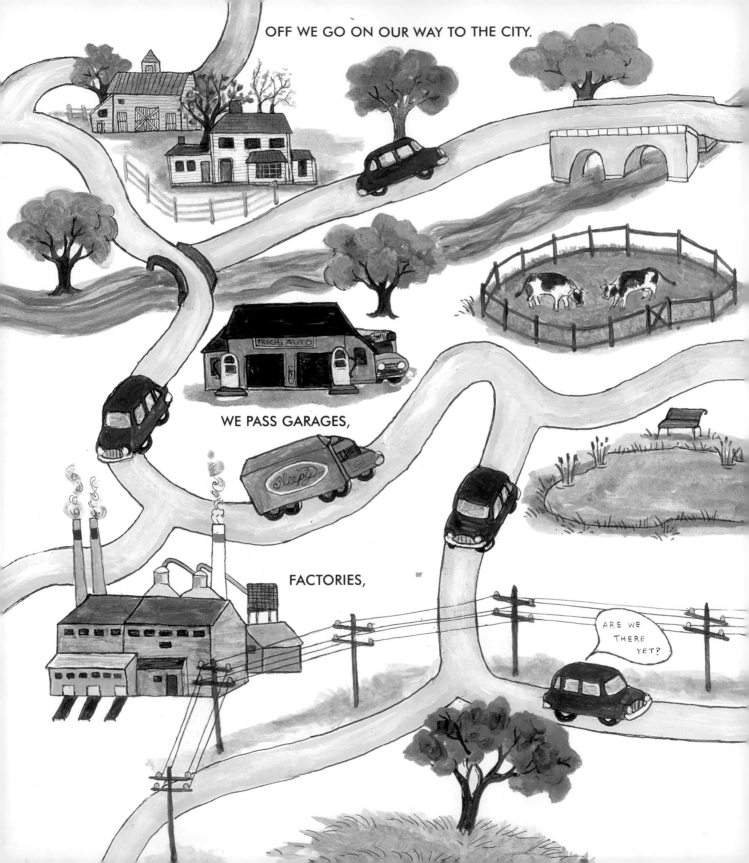

WE PASS
SMALL
VILLAGES,

CHURCHES,

POWER LINES,

PASTURES
AND
FORESTS,

AND HILLS,

GARDENS,

AND FIELDS
AND PONDS.

AND FINALLY THE CITY.

NOTHING BUT CARS AND CONCRETE. YUCK!

OUR CITY FRIENDS MEET US. THEY
ARE TAKING US TO A RESTAURANT
THAT WELCOMES DOGS.

GREAT IDEA!

MAYBE THE CITY ISN'T SO BAD AFTER ALL.

DOG LOVERS' CITY

Canine Cab Co. (Give a Dog a Lift)

Bark-O-Lounge (Dog-Friendly Hotel)

Doggie Bag Heaven Café

Lapdog Luxury Spa

Dog Park

Four-Legged Fashions

Pretty Pooches

Hydrotherapy Heated
Swimming Pool for Pups

THERE ARE SO MANY FUN THINGS TO DO IN THE CITY!

SO MANY
DIFFERENT DOGS
TO BARK AT!

AND AT THE DOG PARK, NO LEASHES!

DOGGIE BOUTIQUE

THE LEASH GOES BACK ON,
BUT WE HEAD TO A GREAT STORE.
NOTHING BUT DOG STUFF!

WHILE MY PEOPLE ARE DECIDING WHAT TO
BUY FOR ME, I WANDER OFF.

OH, LOOK! THERE'S A DOOR TO THE OUTSIDE!

HOORAY!

THE DRIVE HOME SEEMS ENDLESS,
BUT WE MAKE IT WITHOUT ANY PROBLEMS.

AND WE ARE SO HAPPY TO BE BACK ON THE FARM—SAFE AND SOUND!

THE BARN'S NOT A BAD PLACE AFTER ALL.
IT'S WARM AND FRIENDLY AND THERE'S
LOTS OF HAY TO CURL UP IN. SMELLS
GOOD TOO.

DEAR SOCK, GOOD OLD BONE, GOOD
OLD STICK.

SIGH.

GOOD NIGHT.